PRICKLY
TALES

PRICKLY TALES

A Year in the Life of a Young Hedgehog

MARY JOYCE BAXTER

Cover illustration by Kathleen Bulcock

Matador
9 Priory Business Park,
Wistow Road
Kibworth Beauchamp
Leicester LE8 0RX, UK
Tel: (+44) 116 279 2299
Fax: (+44) 116 279 2277
Email: books@troubador.co.uk
Web: www.troubador.co.uk/matador

ISBN 978 1780880 358

British Library Cataloguing in Publication Data.
A catalogue record for this book is available from the British Library.

Typeset by Troubador Publishing Ltd, Leicester, UK

Matador is an imprint of Troubador Publishing Ltd

Printed and bound in the UK by TK International, Padstow, Cornwall

To all the children and staff, past, present and future of
Reedley Hallows Nursery School, Burnley
who have enjoyed these stories.

A First Lesson

Henry was a tiny hedgehog only a few days old. His body was covered with prickles but these were so soft he could snuggle close to his mother to keep warm. He and his sisters were too young to leave the nest their mother had made before they were born.

As the days passed, Henry and his sisters grew bigger and their prickles became longer and more stiff.

Each night, his mother went out to get food. Before she left, she told them not to make any noise.

"Why?" asked Henry.

"Because there are dangers outside. You might get hurt. When you are older I will take you with me."

1

He wanted to go with his mother and scrambled after her. She gave him a push and he slid back into the nest.

"Do keep still," his sisters said. Henry fidgeted so much their bed was disturbed.

"I want to see the world," he said.

"Be quiet or I shall tell mother," said his older sister, Henrietta.

But Henry did not want to be quiet. He felt strong enough to go outside. He peered out from the nest but it was so dark, he could not see anything.

The moon slipped slowly from behind a cloud and Henry blinked. Now he could see much more and it looked exciting. He sniffed the air and put one little paw outside.

"Come and see!" He called to his sisters.

"Don't go out," Henrietta said, "You'll get lost."

Henry did not take any notice and crept out. He thought it would be quiet outside  but he heard strange sounds which scared him. His prickles felt as if they were standing on end as indeed they were.

Suddenly there was a loud noise nearby. It frightened Henry who tried to become as small as possible.

He did not know how it happened, but he found himself rolled into a tight ball. His prickles stood out all over his body and although not very large, they were quite sharp. The dog who had frightened him sniffed at the strange little ball. He yelled as one of Henry's prickles scratched his nose. It was painful and he ran away howling.

Henry kept quite still for a long time, and then tried to stretch himself. It was difficult for he was stuck. He did not know that hedgehogs roll into a ball when there is danger. This is because their prickles stop larger animals from hurting them. He thought his mother would be cross to find him in such a funny position.

He began to worry because the more he tried to stretch, the tighter he got. If he could not unroll he could not eat and he was getting hungry.

The leaves rustled nearby but because his eyes

were tightly shut he could not see what it was.

"Is that you Henry?" his sisters, Henrietta and Hannah were there. "Yes," he whispered.

"What *is* the matter?"

"I don't know. I heard a loud noise and found myself like this."

"What can we do?"

Henry remembered the dog howling. "It was a monster," he said, "I pricked it and it ran away."

"Oh, you are brave," said Hannah.

Henry did not feel brave. He was cold and wanted to stretch his stiff body.

"I want to unroll but I don't know how. Please help me."

Henrietta sniffed carefully around him.

"Hurry up," cried Henry.

Henrietta looked again. She could see a place where his prickles were not so tight.

"I think I've got it," she said.

"Got what?" Henry was feeling tired.

"Take a big breath and breathe out slowly," she said.

Henry did as she said and his body seemed looser.

"Do it again," said Henrietta.

Henry did it again and by the time he had taken his fourth breath he was loose enough to stretch out. Soon they were all back in the nest.

They were worn-out and fell asleep not waking until their mother came home.

"I hope you have been good. That dog was making such a noise; I thought he had found our house."

"We've all been good," said Hannah

"I'll take you out tomorrow," she said, "but first you must learn to be ready for trouble."

Henry did not say anything, which surprised his mother.

"Now all of you, ready for your first lesson?"

"Take a big breath and think that horrid dog is coming."

Henry took a deep breath, thought about the dog and was in a tight ball again.

"That's it Henry. Now Henrietta and Hannah."

Henrietta had several tries before she curled up as well as Henry. Hannah found it harder but at last she too curled up tightly.

Then their mother taught them how to uncurl. Henry, had practised already, and could obey quickly. Henrietta and Hannah were soon as fast as Henry.

"How quickly you learn," remarked their mother.

Henrietta winked at Henry. He was pleased they had not told mother he had been naughty. He smiled and winked back and they all giggled.

"I hope you did not get into mischief while I was out."

"Oh no mother," they replied.

Mother hedgehog stared hard at them but they looked so innocent, she gave them supper and they went to sleep.

Henry Gets Lost

Henry Hedgehog was walking behind his mother and sisters. As he was curious about everything, he stopped to look when he saw something that looked interesting. In a moment he was alone.

..Suddenly the garden seemed full of strange noises. Henry was not very old and everything was new. It was only the second time his mother had taken her family out. He stood still hoping she would come back. Something rustled in the grass. He curled into a tight ball and his prickles stood out to protect him.

"Don't be afraid," he heard a squeaky voice nearby.

Henry unrolled, looked around and blinked. He saw two bright eyes shining in the moonlight. Then he saw a small brown furry animal standing beside him. It had a shiny nose, long whiskers, tiny ears, neat little feet and a long tail.

"Who are you?"

"I'm Willy Wood mouse. I live under that tree over there. I've seen you pass but you didn't notice me."

"I'm sorry, I didn't see you. I'm pleased to meet you."

Henry had been taught to be polite to other animals. That is, when he was sure they meant him no harm.

"When in doubt, curl up, then wait." He could almost hear his mother's words. A tear trickled down his nose. He might never see her again.

"Why are you crying?" Asked Willy.

"I'm lost," sobbed Henry. "I'll never see my mother again."

Don't worry. I know where she is. I know everything that goes on," Willy Woodmouse said kindly.

"Can you take me to her please?"

"Of course I can," replied Willy. "Come with me."

Henry began to feel better. He turned to

follow the little mouse and saw a small brown object on the ground.

"What's that?" He asked sniffing. It smelled nice. He had a nibble. It tasted good and was crunchy. He made a noise as he ate it.

"That was my daytime snack." Willy said. "The humans leave them for birds to eat but we mice like to eat them too. They are called peanuts."

"I'm sorry," said Henry, "but it did taste nice."

"It doesn't matter," Willy said kindly, "but you should ask before eating anything strange. It might not be the right food for you and make you ill."

"I'm sorry." Henry had to say sorry quite often because he was always in trouble. His sisters teased him about it.

Suddenly everything went quiet. They both stood quite still. A shadow passed over the moon.

Henry quickly curled up.

Nothing moved.

Then Willy Woodmouse shook himself and began to

wash his face. "Ooh! That was close." He murmured.

"What was it?" Asked Henry, as he unwound himself.

"It was an owl. An enemy of mine. They like to eat mice. We have to watch for them all the time. It wouldn't hurt you because of your prickles. It lives up in that tree."

"Oh," said Henry. "Do I have any enemies?"

"Not many. Only the monsters on the road. Most animals don't like your prickles because they hurt."

Henry gave a sigh of relief.

Against the brown earth, Henry's small brown body was difficult to see. His eyes shone like stars from his dark brown head. His prickles were a lighter brown and hairs of a lighter brown colour ran from his small ears and below his prickles. When he ran, his legs worked like a clockwork toy as he raised his body away from the ground.

Last years' leaves rustled and he stopped to scatter them. It was fun!

Willy urged him on. "Hurry up; your mother will be worried."

They scurried through the flowerbeds.

Splash! Henry fell into the pond. He was not watching where Willy Woodmouse was leading him.

"Ooh! Aah! Help! "He shouted for the water was cold.

Willy turned in surprise but now Henry was swimming happily.

"Look at me! I can swim." He yelled from the water. "Come in too."

"No thanks." Willy shuddered, "Don't make so much noise."

Henry scrambled out shaking water from his prickles.

Willy dodged the drops. It was hard work looking after young hedgehogs.

 They entered the vegetable patch. Henry saw three dark  shadows, one large and two smaller ones.

"It's my mother and sisters." Henry ran

towards them. "Oh I'm glad I've found you."

His mother gave him a nudge with her nose. "I knew you would not be lost for long. Everyone in the garden is so helpful." She smiled at Willy. "It was kind of you. Was he much trouble?"

"Not at all. Glad to help. Goodbye!" With a wave, Willy was gone.

"Where have you been?" Hannah sounded cross.

"I've been having fun and found a new friend"

"You should stay with us," Henrietta said.

"Yes. Stay close until you are older," said his mother.

Henry smiled to himself. It had been a lovely adventure. He had been frightened at first. Then the water had been cold but now he knew how to swim and it was fun.

He was glad Willy Woodmouse had helped him. When he grew up, he would look after himself. Then he would do all sorts of exciting things and have even more adventures.

A Strange Dream

Henry had been looking for food with his mother. He was tired but although it was getting quite light, he did not want to go to bed. Hedgehogs look for food at night and by morning, are ready to sleep but Henry wanted to stay up longer. Mother hedgehog tried to make him go to bed but he would rather watch the sun come into the garden.

His mother was glad when the night ended but worried when he stayed outside until it was light.

"Light is bad for you," she told him, "it's not safe if it's very bright."

"Why isn't it safe?" asked Henry.

"Because there are monsters out there who

make a loud noise and have two very bright eyes which can see everything."

"Why must I stay in the dark?" He said.

"Because," his mother said. "Your uncle once went to look at those bright lights. We never saw him again."

Henry sighed. It was not much fun being young. When he was grown up he would do exciting things. He would meet Willy Woodmouse again but his mother watched him carefully since he had been lost.

"Why can't I go and talk to Willy Woodmouse?" he asked.

"Because Willy is busy. He has no time for chattering."

Henry gave a yawn and blinked. The light was getting brighter.

"Come on now. Time to sleep," his mother called again.

Henry went slowly to bed.

Soon he was fast asleep on his bed of dry leaves and grass.

When Henry woke, it was dark for it was night again. Except for the wind murmuring in the trees everything was quiet. His mother and sisters were still asleep. He felt lively and did not want to wait for them.

Carefully, he crept into the garden. He scurried along the path and stopped to eat a little slug. He knew these were good for hedgehogs. His mother said they would make his prickles grow strong.

"The humans like you to eat slugs too," his mother had said. "The more slugs we eat, the less there are to eat their garden plants."

Henry thought it was fun being on his own. He wondered why his mother worried. He could look after himself now he was almost grown up. He came to a wide open space where the ground was very hard.

Suddenly he heard a buzzing noise. As if all the bees in the world were hunting for honey. His mother knew about bees because sometimes they saw them on their way home before it got really dark.

"Leave them alone and they won't hurt you," mother said. "Bees are frightened if you disturb them. Then they sting, which is very painful."

But this noise was louder. Henry thought

his ears would burst. He saw two bright lights, shut his eyes tight and rolled into a prickly ball. Then the lights were gone and he heard only a faint hum in the distance. He started to explore again. He had not gone far when he heard the strange noise again. Two glaring eyes came out of nowhere. He tried to run to get out of the way but did not know which way to go.

In a moment it was over. A bump and Henry lay in the road wondering what had  happened. It felt as if all his breath had been squashed out of him.

When he tried to get up he could not move. He tried to shout but no sound came. Henry had been run over by a motor car.

Far away, he heard voices and tried to hear what they were saying. He was really frightened now as he lay and gasped. Then he recognised Willy Woodmouse's squeaky voice. "Oh dear. It's Henry. He's been run over. What shall we do?" The voice sounded very worried.

"Ooh. He's flat as a pancake," another squeaky voice spoke.

"He looks like one too," someone giggled.

There were squeaks all around.

"We can't leave him here," said Willy.

"Now then everyone,

when I say heave, we all push him onto his side, then we roll him home."

There was a lot of heaving and pushing. Henry tried to see what was happening but he was surrounded by the little mice.

Then he was being rolled over the ground. It was horribly bumpy. He heard gasps and squeaks that suddenly seemed far away. He was rolling down the garden path at a tremendous speed. Bump! He hit the trunk of the old apple tree and gave a scream.

"Now, now," it was his mother's voice. "You rolled out of bed into the tree. You've been dreaming. Your bed is squashed flat."

Henry told his mother about the dream.

"Willy Woodmouse is always helpful," she said. "Even in dreams."

Later, she reminded Henry about the monsters which rushed along outside the garden. They were very dangerous. All the animals kept far away from them.

"I'm glad it was only a dream," she said with a smile.

"So am I," said Henry with a sigh. He kept close to his mother that night and did not argue with his sisters for a long time.

The Real Road

Early one evening, Henry saw Willy Woodmouse and told him about his dream. Willy could not help laughing when he heard about Henry being flat as a pancake.
"It wasn't funny," said Henry. "I was frightened and dizzy when I rolled down the path."

"You must have dreamed about a road," said Willy.

"What's is a road like?" asked Henry.

"It's like a river."

"What's a river?"

A river is a lot of moving water. Sometimes it rushes very quickly."

"How do you know about rivers?"

"Some of my cousins live near rivers. It's hard to swim in them when they move fast. It's best not to go too near."

"I wonder why I dreamed about the road," said Henry.

Willy sat up and cleaned his whiskers. "I saw the road when my House Mice cousins came."

"Are they like you?"

"Not as good looking as we Wood Mice. They didn't stay long. They ate all my food, then said it was too quiet here and went home."

Henry thought about this for a moment, then said, "I'm glad my cousins don't come to stay."

The moon rose over the trees and the shadows became deeper.

"My mother will be here soon. Tell me about the road."

"I was sitting in the bushes when I saw it. So big and wide, I couldn't see the other side. There were big noisy monsters going up and down along it."

"Ooh, were you frightened?"

"No. I was in the bushes so they couldn't see me. I saw the children too."

"Whose children? Yours?"

"No. These were human two legged

children. They stood by the road and looked one way, then they looked the other way. When the monsters stopped, they walked across."

"They must be brave," said Henry.

"One of the monsters came into the garden but it came very slowly. It swallowed some of the children but they didn't seem to mind. I could hear them laughing as it ran away with them."

"I wouldn't like that at all," said Henry.

The bushes rustled and Henry's mother and sisters appeared.

"Remember and look both ways before you try to cross over a road," warned Willy as he disappeared into the bushes.

"What was Willy talking about?" asked Henrietta.

"He was telling me about roads."

"What are roads? she asked.

"I'll tell you sometime," said Henry.

"You are now old enough to find food on your own." said mother.

"What fun," replied Henry.

"Just be careful," she said. "Don't get into trouble."

This was great, thought Henry, now he

could look for the real road and see if it was like the dream one.

He hurried further along the garden path and found himself on a wide hard piece of ground. A strange creature was standing there. It had four feet which smelled strange but it stood quietly, not making any noise.

"That's one of the monsters I told you about." Willy Woodmouse popped up beside him. "The road is just here."

Henry followed eagerly.

The road was just as he had seen it in his dream. It shone in the moonlight but was quiet with no monsters to be seen. Henry stepped onto it.

"Stop!" cried Willy.

"Why? asked Henry but he did stop.

"Look," said Willy.

Henry looked. Two huge glaring eyes seemed to be coming straight towards him. Henry curled quickly into a ball.

"Don't do that," shouted Willy. "That way you might get squashed and *I* can't roll you home by myself."

Henry undid himself. "What should I do then?"

"Look both ways first, then go over as fast as you can to the other side when no more monsters are coming."

"Thank you," said Henry.

Henry looked first one way and then the other. He saw the bright lights in the distance and waited until they had gone. Then he hurried to the middle of the road but was dismayed to see another monster coming towards him.

Should he run back or go on?

Henry decided to go on over to the other side. The monster rushed by, the wind rushed through his prickles but he was safe.

On the other side of the road he found another garden with lots of delicious food to eat.

Henry stayed there all night, eating and snuffling around. He liked this garden but decided to go back where he had lived all his life and find his sisters.

He looked both ways very carefully when he came to the road. It was quiet now with no gleaming eyed monsters anywhere. He crossed to the familiar smells of his own garden. It was time for sleeping for the first birds were waking and starting their morning song.

"Where have you been Henry?" The voice came from the side of the lawn and Henry turned to see his sisters in the bushes.

"I've had an adventure and found another garden."

"Tell me about it ," said Henrietta.

"Later, perhaps," said Henry, "I'm tired and full of food. Lets go to bed."

The three small hedgehogs walked across the lawn to find a comfortable place to sleep. They curled up among last years dry leaves under a bush. Their mother passed by and was pleased to see they were safe and sound.

The Hognapping

One summer night, Henry was out early before it was really dark. He was snuffling around looking for things to eat when he saw a round object. It moved when he touched it with his nose.

What could it be? He pushed it but it ran away.

"Who are you?" he asked.

There was no reply.

It was no use trying to make friends with something that did not answer so Henry went on looking for food Suddenly there was a noise close by as someone ran down the path. Henry curled into a prickly ball for safety.

Something touched him and he heard a loud shriek.

What could it be? Henry rolled up more tightly.

Soon he heard more noises and voices just above him.

"Why it's only a hedgehog," said a deep human voice.

"But it bit me," another shrill voice insisted. "I thought it was my ball and tried to pick it up."

"You must have touched its prickles. It  wouldn't hurt you. Hedgehogs are good to have in the garden."

"Why?"

"Because they eat lots of slugs and other things."

"Ugh."

"You might not think them nice but hedgehogs enjoy them."

"Can we keep him if we find somewhere for him to sleep," it was a girl's voice this time.

"Only a few days as we should not keep wild things prisoner."

Without warning, Henry was lifted into the air. It made him dizzy and he struggled to get away. It was no use and he couldn't curl into a ball because the hands were under his body. Just when he thought this was the end of the world they let go.

But where was he? It was strange and as he snuffled around to find a way out, some dried grass was thrown on top of him. "Don't smother him," the deep voice said.

"I didn't mean to hurt him."

"You frightened him, remember he probably hasn't seen people before."

Henry heard the voices rumbling above him but couldn't understand the words. He was worried and curled into a tight ball.

The children had put him into a wooden box. He kept very still until everything seemed quiet.

Very slowly, Henry uncurled and sniffed. There was something with him. The humans had placed food close by. He sniffed and took a nibble. It was not as nice as the food in the garden so he pushed it away.

He felt so lonely and wondered where his friends were. He gave a sob wondering if he would ever see them again. Next he tried to find a way to escape. It was no use, so after walking round and round for most of the night, he went to sleep.

Next morning, Roger came to look at Henry.

"He didn't eat the food. It's spilt everywhere," he said.

"Take it away then and give him something fresh tonight."

Henry heard other voices because more children had come to look at him.

"What have you called him?" said one.

"Henry," said the little girl.

"I think you should call him Prickles," said one of the boys.

"Can I hold him?"

"Let Me. Oh. Ouch."

When the boys went away, Henry slowly uncurled and stretched because he ached from being rolled up tightly for so long.

Then they brought more food but Henry tasted and then left it.

"Perhaps he doesn't like bread and milk," said Roger. "I'll ask my teacher what to give him."

The day went by slowly. Henry's tummy rumbled because it was empty. He ate some of the bread and milk but it gave him a tummy pain so he curled up and went to sleep.

He was wakened by voices again.

"My teacher said that bread and milk gives hedgehogs tummy ache so it's better to give them puppy food."

Something nearby smelled good. Henry stretched and took a nibble. It was not as nice as fresh food but better than that other stuff.

"My teacher said hedgehogs were wild creatures and shouldn't be kept prisoner," said Sally. "Shall we let him go."

"That would be best. You can put food out every night and he'll know you're his friend."

"Yes let's do that," said Roger, "but first I'll put a mark on his back so I can recognise him if I see him again."

He went away and Henry felt something being rubbed on his prickles. After this he was taken out of the box and taken to the same spot where he had been when he was captured. He kept still for a long time but at last the wonderful smell of the garden made him feel happy.

"I'm free. I'm free." he shouted.

"Who is making all that noise?"

Henry saw Hannah coming across the grass.

"Whatever happened to you? Not another adventure?"

"I suppose it was but it was not very nice."

"Will you tell me about it?" said Hannah.

"Perhaps," said Henry, "I'm hungry now, I want some food."

Henry did not forget his adventure and soon decided that humans were not so bad after all. Every night, close to the place where he had been hognapped, he found a dish of food. This was good for when the weather grew colder, his own food became scarce. He was glad of the extra supply.

More Danger

One evening in late summer, Henry wandered through the garden. He wanted to find the puppy food the children always put out for him but when he reached the place, the food had gone. He looked up and saw two luminous green eyes glaring at him. Henry rolled up quickly. His mother had said cats rarely bothered hedgehogs but it was better to be careful.

It was easier to get into the nearby gardens now and there were plenty of new areas to visit. The childrens' father had made places in the fence and hedge around the garden. This was so the hedgehogs could wander further and not be in danger from the road.

After he had eaten some tasty slugs and beetles, Henry went to explore outside the garden. He found a gap he had not seen before and carefully went through.

As he walked along, Henry found himself in another garden which was rather overgrown. It looked as if it might be a good place to forage for food when he was hungry. He soon found himself near a strange house and could hear loud music being played. There might be humans there so he turned to go back to his own garden.

Suddenly the delightful smell of puppy food made his nose twitch eagerly. He loved the puppy food the children put out for him. Tonight he had been too late and the cat had eaten it all. Perhaps other people were putting out food too. He hurried to find it but all he found was an almost empty tin of food lying under a bush. Henry pushed his nose into the tin to get the scraps of food and suddenly found his head stuck tight.

The children in his own garden were always careful to flatten empty food tins and put them in the bin. Earlier in the day, someone had put this tin in their dustbin but had not flattened it. When the bin was emptied, it fell out. No one noticed and it rolled under a bush where it lay all day.

Henry was in great danger as he tried to get rid of the tin. It would not move because his prickles were stuck in the rim. When he tried to pull his head out, his prickles pulled in the wrong direction. It was very painful and he was frightened. He ran round and round in terror. This was the worst thing that had ever happened to him.

He shook his head but this made it worse. He could not see where he was going as he ran in panic towards the road which was quite close. Suddenly he stopped with a thump as he bumped into the gatepost. It hurt so much that Henry saw stars all around him. Now he was running towards the road and as his head was inside the tin could not see two bright car headlights in the distance.

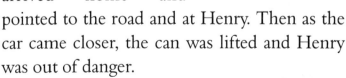

Roger's father had just arrived home and pointed to the road and at Henry. Then as the car came closer, the can was lifted and Henry was out of danger.

"Is it Henry?" asked Roger who had been

waiting for his father and was so glad a hedgehog had been saved.

"I don't know but I must get him out of this," he said.

Henry was struggling more than ever. He was held gently and the voices were quiet as they talked to him.

"Hold his body firmly," Roger was told. "Then I'll ease the tin off."

First a big duster was wrapped round Henry's body. Then he found something flat to ease carefully under the tin to flatten Henry's prickles.

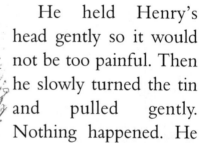

He held Henry's head gently so it would not be too painful. Then he slowly turned the tin and pulled gently. Nothing happened. He tried again but this time pulled a little harder. With a little pop, Henry's head came out. Some of his prickles were bent and some broken but he was safe. He lay in the boy's hands gasping and blinking in the light. It felt so good to breathe properly again.

"It *is* Henry. Look there's the mark I put on

him last month when we hognapped him."

The boy gave Henry a stroke and took him into the garden. His father brought out some fresh puppy food which Henry enjoyed.

"I'm glad we found you," he said as Henry ate some of the food before hurrying away.

The boy's father made sure the tin was quite flat before he put it into their own collection bin.

"I'll tell everyone at school to be extra careful with tins," said Roger. "It could have been really nasty for Henry if we hadn't seen him.

Henry, who was now safe in his own garden, would have agreed with him.

The next day, Roger told the teacher what had happened. The teacher asked him to tell the rest of the class.

"It was good that my father was later home than usual and rescued Henry or he might have been run over," he told them. We knew it was the same hedgehog because of the yellow paint I put on his back. He didn't like it when I did it but now we know him we can try and keep him safe."

Henry Finds Himself in Prison

It had been a hot summer day, so hot, Henry left his sleeping place in the bushes to try and get cool. Life was easier because the humans put food out every night and he was getting lazy.

As he was enjoying some of the food, he looked up and saw two luminous green eyes glaring at him. Henry rolled up quickly.

When everything was quiet, Henry unrolled and was annoyed because all the food had gone. He hurried away to hunt food for himself in the shrubbery.

After he had eaten Henry went to explore outside the garden. He set off along the side of the road stopping now and then to eat a small slug or beetle. The moon made shadows but Henry was alone. There were no houses just stone walls because he had reached the countryside.

A dog barked but the sound seemed far away so he went on walking.

Suddenly, the ground gave way under Henry's feet and he felt himself falling through the air. As he dropped, he curled up and his prickles acted like a cushion as he landed with a bounce.

He opened his eyes slowly. Everything was dark and he felt frightened. A long way above, he saw iron bars outlined against the night sky. He was in some sort of prison. This was not a pleasant adventure.

Henry looked for a way out. He walked all round his prison. There were steep walls on every side and no way of escape.

"What can I do?" He asked himself.

It was very quiet and there was no food there. Henry's tummy rumbled because he felt hungry. He sat down and scratched himself. The fleas hiding in his prickles were also hungry.

"Help, help," he called, but no one heard.

A small beetle scurried past and Henry grabbed it eagerly. He would need more than

37

one little beetle to keep alive he thought.

"Suppose I never get out," he thought.
Henry walked backwards and forwards and
round and round until he was dizzy. There was
no way out. At last, he went to sleep.

He woke in the morning and now he could
see where he was. Although Henry did not
know its name, it was a cattle grid, which is
made to stop cows and sheep wandering from
the moorlands.

Again, he tried but still could not find a way
to escape.

Then he heard voices. It was Saturday
morning and the children were going to the
farm for eggs.

One little boy was swishing a stick at the grass.
It hit a hidden stone and fell out of his hand
almost falling into the cattle grid. As he stooped
to pick it up, his eyes opened in amazement.

"Look what I've found," he shouted.

The others turned back.

"Why it's the hedgehog from our garden," one of them said.

"How do you know? All hedgehogs look alike," said another.

"It's because of the yellow spot on his back. I put it there."

"He must have fallen down there."

"We must get him out."

"There's an old floor board in our shed. I'll get it."

He dashed away soon returning with the wood. Carefully pushing it through the metal bars, they made a ramp.

"That should make it easy for him to get out" the girl said.

"I'll stay and watch," said the smallest boy.

The others went on to the farm.

Henry saw the strange object at the end of his prison. When everywhere was quiet, he crept over and sniffed. It seemed harmless. He sniffed again. It did not move when he placed his front feet on it. Henry walked up slowly to the top where he smelled cool fresh air.

He heaved himself into the road, his little nose quivered happily. Now out of prison he blinked in the bright light. Hedgehogs are not used to daylight so he wanted to find a place to sleep.

Trying to find his way out during the night, Henry had walked in so many directions, now he was completely lost. He turned this way and that way, sniffing the air, not at all sure where to go. He heard the childrens' voices as they returned from the farm and curled up.

"Oh good, he's out," said one.

"I don't think he knows which way to go," said another boy.

"Well let's take him with us back to the garden."

Carefully, they took the eggs from the bag and lifted Henry into it. The girl carried Henry and the others carried the eggs. In his own garden, they placed him under a bush.

When it was quiet, Henry opened his eyes and recognised the old apple tree nearby. With a happy sigh, he stretched out and went to sleep.

When the boys went to fetch the piece of wood, the farmer was there.

"This was a good idea of yours," he said. "I'm going to make a ramp in case other hedgehogs fall in."

The children decided to ask everyone to make their cattle grids safe.

Bonfire Night

At the end of October, the first frosts came to the garden. Henry Hedgehog found a place to sleep through the cold days of winter. It was at the bottom of the garden under a pile of rubbish the children had collected to make a bonfire on Guy Fawkes Night.

By now, Henry was grownup and quite fat with all the food he had eaten. He went to sleep in his nest of dried grass. His breathing was so slow it looked as if he was not breathing at all. This is a special kind of sleep called hibernation. It is how some animals are able to live through the cold winter when there is not much food for them. When spring comes they are quite thin as they have used all the food stored as fat in their bodies.

This was Henry's first winter but he had chosen a bad place to sleep. The little woodmice who scurried around collecting food for their winter store did not know or they might have warned him.

The squirrel, who built his nest high in the branches of a chestnut tree did not know. He was trying to remember where his nuts and acorns were hidden.

Even the shouts of the children as they piled more wood on the bonfire, did not wake Henry. They were pleased with the Guy they had made and were eager to place it on the top.

The afternoon was bright and sunny. The warm sun penetrated through to the dry warm nest and made Henry feel less sleepy. He heard the shouts of the children and wondered what was going on but was too sleepy to move.

The children were waiting impatiently for their father to light the bonfire.

"We are not going to light the bonfire until after tea," he said as he came into the garden.

"Why not? We want to light it now," the voices clamoured.

"There is something very important to do first," he said.

"What's more important than lighting the bonfire?"

"Your friend Henry Hedgehog might have decided that our pile of rubbish would make an ideal place to spend the winter.'"

The children were horrified. "Oh no. He might get burned," they said.

"Not if we move everything first. Come on, it won't take long."

"What will we do if we find Henry down there?"

"There's a dry place under the shed. Put some dry leaves and grass ready just in case," their father instructed.

Everyone worked hard and when it was almost dark, one of the children ran indoors to get a torch.

"I hope we find him," said one little girl.

"If he's there we will."

At last, nearly all the rubbish had been moved and right in the middle they could see the round prickly ball that was Henry. Very carefully, so he would not be disturbed too much, the man pushed a small spade under him, lifted it up and carried him to the shed.

After pushing in the grass and leaves, he

gently moved the spade with Henry on it under the shed as far as it would go. Then he raised the handle so that Henry would slide off and into his new home.

"That's my seaside spade," said the little girl.

"Yes, its been very useful," replied her father.

Henry was forgotten as they danced around

the bonfire and ate baked potatoes and chestnuts.

"These are good," they said.

After the disturbance, Henry was not as sleepy as before. Soon he smelled the smoke and wondered what was happening.

When he opened his eyes, he did not know where he was. This was not the nest he had made a few days ago. He scraped and tugged at the leaves and grass until his bed was comfortable.

After this, he became curious and crept quietly into the garden.

There was a strange smell which he did not like very much. It was bright outside but not the same as daytime. He looked for his old home and saw that it had been moved.

Something strange had happened for now it was burning and was very hot as the sparks flew skyward. Henry was afraid to go too close.

"What's happening?" he thought. "Is this a dream?"

Then he remembered he had a new place to sleep which was just as nice as his old home but safer. As he turned to go, he saw hundreds of stars glittering in the sky and all around him.

It was wonderful; Henry forgot his cold feet as he stood under the apple tree watching the fireworks. It was lovely and he wanted it to last forever. Suddenly there was a loud bang close by, then another and another. This was dreadful and Henry's heart began to pound.

He turned and ran as fast as his little legs would move.

Luckily the shed was near and he curled up tightly in his new home. His heartbeats slowed down as he settled into his deep hibernation sleep.

Christmas

In the middle of December, the weather which had been mild suddenly turned cold and frosty. One morning, the children woke up and saw everything in the garden was white. They had fun building a snow man and rolling huge snow balls over the lawn. They hoped the snow would last until Christmas.

In his cosy bed, Henry did not hear them or know about the snow. His breathing was slow and because he did not need much energy, his heart beats were also slow.

"I wonder if Henry is nice and warm?" said one of the children as the snowball he had thrown hit the shed where Henry was sleeping.

"Don't wake him," said the little girl.

"He's missing all the fun."

"I'm sure he doesn't mind" said their mother bringing hot drinks. "I wonder if we shall have a white Christmas?"

"We can play with the snow in the holidays if we do."

A few days later, the snow began to thaw and the weather was much warmer. The sun came our during the day and warmed the ground.

Henry felt the change and began to wake up. He stretched and yawned before peering out into the garden. It was dark and quiet so he decided to take a walk. He felt hungry and thought something to eat would be welcome.

Giving another stretch, he ventured out.

All through the winter, the children had been putting food out just in case Henry woke and felt hungry. Some nights it disappeared and they were not sure whether it was eaten by Henry or the cat from next door. Tonight, Henry enjoyed the food before going back to his bed.

When he'd finished, he walked down the garden path towards his home. As he did so, the children and their parents arrived home from the Christmas Concert.

"I'm sure that's Henry," said Sally.

"It can't be," said her brother.

They shone a torch and were just in time to see Henry turn the corner and disappear from sight.

"It *was* Henry. Happy Christmas Henry," said the girl.

"Don't be silly, hedgehogs don't have a Christmas." her brother laughed.

"Yes they do. Henry will have a Christmas, won't he?"

"I'm sure he will," replied her mother. "Now children, get to bed quickly or Santa Claus won't come."

The children hurried off but the little girl stayed behind.

"Will Henry have some Christmas dinner?"

"We'll have to see what happens tomorrow."

Soon the children were fast asleep and their parents were busy getting things ready before they, too went to bed.

In the morning, the children had great fun opening their presents.

The little girl had not forgotten Henry and reminded her mother about him.

"Perhaps Henry will come for his supper tonight."

"Yes, he might," said her mother.

"What can we give him for a special treat?"

"We mustn't give him anything that might make him ill."

"Would he like some nuts?"

"We could give him some pieces of nut to try with his

puppyfood."

The little girl found a brazil nut, a hazel nut and some cloth which she tried to stitch into something which looked like a small stocking.

"It's for his Christmas presents," she explained.

"Hedgehogs don't have presents," laughed her brother.

"Henry does," she said.

Later they crept into the garden and left the food in the usual place. Afterwards they waited quietly for they did not want to frighten Henry. The weather was dry but seemed colder than it had been on Christmas Eve.

"It might be too cold for him," whispered the boys.

"Please come for your Christmas things," said the girl.

There was a rustle as Henry made his way towards the food. He sniffed, then nibbled at the brazil nut which he seemed to enjoy. Leaving him, they crept into the house to get warm again.

"Perhaps Henry will go back into his hibernation sleep after this," said one of the boys.

"We'll still put out food, won't we?" asked the girl.

"Of course we will even if the cat does eat some of it,"

Just before bedtime, they crept out again to see if Henry had finished his food. The dish was empty and he had left nut crumbs everywhere for the birds to tidy up in the morning. The little stocking was nowhere to be seen.

In his bed, Henry felt comfortable and full of food. He'd dragged the piece of cloth in and it felt comfortable among the leaves and grass in his bed. He gave a big contented sigh as he stretched himself and had a little scratch.

It was quiet outside as a few flakes of snow fell on the garden. Perhaps Henry would sleep now until the worst of the winter frosts ended.

Spring was still many months away but the children were pleased Henry was safe. If the weather did get warm enough to wake him, there would always be food for him. This would help him to survive through the winter to see another year and more adventures.

Springtime

It was a long, cold winter. In his deep hibernation sleep, Henry did not know what was happening outside. Towards the end of March, the weather grew warmer. In the garden, crocuses pushed through the soil to parade in colourful masses across the lawn and in the borders.

There was a different feeling in the air. Henry's nose twitched as he woke and became aware of the world around. He stretched and took his first steps of the year. He wanted to skip and jump but hedgehogs can't do this.

Slowly he crept out of his nest and sniffed. New scents made him want to explore. He breathed in the air and felt very hungry. It was a long time since he had last eaten. During his long sleep, all the fat in his body had been used to keep him alive and now he was quite thin.

"I must find something to eat," he thought.

He'd forgotten about the food usually left by the children. Then his nose twitched as he smelled the food and remembered where it would be. It was delicious and he ate greedily, then went for a walk through the garden.

Spikey leaves pushing through the soil as bulbs squeezed into the light. Slugs and beetles were appearing now the weather was warmer and Henry enjoyed eating them.

It was wonderful to be awake and enjoy the freshness of springtime. Memories returned of things that happened the year before. He found last years pathways. He wanted to explore but felt tired and went home to rest.

Each day, he grew stronger and put on more weight. Now he was quite grown up and as big as he would grow.

During the days that followed, sometimes he met other hedgehogs but hurried on his way. Hedgehogs like to be alone except when young. Then they stay close to their mothers until they are able to find their own food.

One evening Henry woke up with a very peculiar feeling. His prickles were tingling in a strange way and he did not know why. They tingled when he went into the garden. On the path he met another hedgehog and his prickles tingled even more. This was a new experience for Henry for this was a lady hedgehog. She was called Holly because she was as prickly as a holly bush.

"Don't go," he called and hurried after her.

He found himself getting very breathless and his voice made huffing and puffing noises. Henry had fallen in love. Holly stopped for a moment before moving into the bushes.

Together they wandered through the garden eating juicy pieces of food. Every now and again Henry huffed and puffed at her but it was just his way of telling her how much he liked her.

When morning came, they went to their own nests. In the evening, Henry's prickles did not tingle any more and he hardly noticed Holly when they passed on the lawn. He did not know that soon she would be busy preparing for the arrival of her own family. She would not notice Henry any more.

Over the next weeks, Henry met other lady hedgehogs and found his prickles tingling many times during those spring days.

Although he did not know, the day came when Henry was more than one year old. He now knew every secret place and where the best food could be found. One night he was almost pushed to one side of the path as a line of hedgehogs passed by. It was Holly and her family hurrying behind their mother. Henry gazed in amazement at his own children. Could he have been as small, he wondered. Just then, the last little hedgehog stopped to sniff at something in the grass.

"That's the way to get lost," said Henry as he pushed the little one gently back into line before going on  his way. He remembered the trouble he had caused his own mother when he was small His sister Henrietta often came to his rescue and he had been grateful.

To a small new hedgehog, the world is full of danger. He knew. Now he realised how much his mother had taught him.

He no longer curled into a ball when the children came to look for him. Sometimes he stayed still until they had gone. Sometimes he sniffed at their feet before going to eat the food they continued to leave. He always curled up tightly when he heard the dog or saw the cat from next door. They were not to be trusted and he kept away from the places they liked. Now he had no problems in unrolling himself and often laughed about the time he got stuck.

He had not seen his sisters since he had gone to sleep for the winter. They had both gone to live in other gardens. If they had met, he would not have recognised them. Soon they too would have families of their own.

It seemed a long time since Henry was a small hedgehog who was always in mischief. During his first year so many things had happened. Now at last he was grown up and felt able to take care of himself. He did not know that his world still held many dangers for small creatures and would go on learning for the rest of his life..